12/2015

Jon Scieszka's TRUCKTOWN

KAT'S MAPS

WRITTEN BY JON SCIESZKA

CHARACTERS AND ENVIRONMENTS DEVELOPED BY THE

DAVID SHANNON   **LOREN LONG**   **DAVID GORDON**

ILLUSTRATION CREW:

Executive Producer:

TOT
INDUSTRIES

Creative Supervisor: Nina Rappaport Brown ◐ Drawings by: Dan Root ◐ Color by: Antonio Reyna

Art Director: Laura Roode

READY-TO-READ

SIMON SPOTLIGHT

NEW YORK   LONDON   TORONTO   SYDNEY

ABDO

Spotlight

ABDOPUBLISHING.COM

Reinforced library bound edition published in 2016 by Spotlight,
a division of ABDO. PO Box 398166, Minneapolis, Minnesota 55439.
Spotlight produces high-quality reinforced library bound editions for
schools and libraries. Published by agreement with Simon Spotlight.

Printed in the United States of America, North Mankato, Minnesota.
042015   092015

SIMON SPOTLIGHT

An imprint of Simon & Schuster Children's Publishing Division
1230 Avenue of the Americas, New York, NY 10020
First Simon Spotlight edition February 2011
Copyright © 2011 by JRS Worldwide, LLC. TRUCKTOWN AND JON SCIESZKA'S
TRUCKTOWN and design are trademarks of JRS Worldwide, LLC. All rights reserved,
including the right of reproduction in whole or in part in any form. SIMON SPOTLIGHT,
READY-TO-READ, and colophon are registered trademarks of Simon & Schuster, Inc.

LIBRARY OF CONGRESS CATALOGING-IN-PUBLICATION DATA

This title was previously cataloged with the following information:

Scieszka, Jon.
  Kat's maps / by Jon Scieszka ; artwork created by The Design Garage: David Gordon,
Loren Long, David Shannon. — 1st Simon Spotlight ed.
  p. cm. — (Jon Scieszka's Trucktown) (Ready-to-read)
Summary: Kat, who loves to make maps of all sorts of places and things, gives a special
map to Jack.
[1. Maps—Fiction. 2. Drawing—Fiction.] I. Design Garage. II. Title.
PZ7.S41267Kas 2011
[E]—dc22
                              2009046920

978-1-61479-395-3 (reinforced library bound edition)

ABDO **Spotlight**   A Division of ABDO   abdopublishing.com

Kat makes maps
of her room,

maps of her block,

my house

flower box

N

maps of her town,

and maps of her world.

Kat loves maps.

Kat makes maps of her mind

and maps of her heart.

"Here is a map for you,"
says Kat to Jack.

"Where does it go?"

"To a surprise."

Jack follows Kat's map.

He turns right on Bumper Street.

He turns left on Motor Lane.

Jack drives over Speed Highway.

Under Race Bridge.

"Aha," says Jack.

"I should have guessed."

"An art show of all . . .

". . . Kat's maps."